T0113863

# Jesus's Echo

## S. M. Rath

WESTBOW
PRESS®
A DIVISION OF THOMAS NELSON
& ZONDERVAN

WestBow Press books may be ordered through
booksellers or by contacting:

WestBow Press
A Division of Thomas Nelson & Zondervan
1663 Liberty Drive
Bloomington, IN 47403
www.westbowpress.com
844-714-3454

Because of the dynamic nature of the Internet, any web addresses or
links contained in this book may have changed since publication and
may no longer be valid. The views expressed in this work are solely those
of the author and do not necessarily reflect the views of the publisher,
and the publisher hereby disclaims any responsibility for them.

Any people depicted in stock imagery provided by Getty Images are models,
and such images are being used for illustrative purposes only.
Certain stock imagery © Getty Images.

Scripture quotations marked NKJV are taken from the
New King James Version. Copyright © 1982 by Thomas
Nelson, Inc. Used by permission. All rights reserved.

ISBN: 978-1-6642-9005-1 (sc)
ISBN: 978-1-6642-9006-8 (e)

Library of Congress Control Number: 2023901344

Print information available on the last page.

WestBow Press rev. date:   01/31/2023

For all the soldiers who keep America safe
and protect our freedoms today
and in loving memory of my father,
John Junior, who did the same during WWII.

◆

For God has not given us a spirit of fear,
but of power and of love and of a sound mind.
*2 Timothy 1:7 NKJV*

# CONTENTS

# CHAPTER 1

## Noah and His Father

Kneeling on the floor in front of the coffee table, Noah emptied his box of toy soldiers. The green, plastic figures scattered across the wooden surface in disarray.

As Noah arranged his toy soldiers, he thought about being a *real* soldier someday. His father was a real soldier. His father was a soldier in the United States Army.

A short time later, Noah's father entered the room, carrying his Bible. "Hi, Noah," he said. "What are you doing?"

Noah smiled at his father. "I'm playing with my soldiers. Someday, I'm going to be a real soldier, just like you, Daddy."

"That's very honorable of you," Noah's father said. Noah's father then sat on the couch, placed his Bible beside him, and asked his son, "Do you know why I wanted to be a soldier?"

Noah proudly answered, "Because you love our country."

"That's right," Noah's father said, smiling. "But do you know *why* I love our country?"

"Um . . ." Noah started to say. He was not sure why his father loved their county. Only that his father did.

Noah's father patted the cushion beside him on the couch. "Will you sit with me?" he asked Noah.

Noah grabbed his favorite toy soldier and then sat on the couch beside his father. His father was a big, strong man, and Noah always felt safe when he was with his father.

"I love our country," Noah's father began, "because in our country we are free. Everyone who lives here is free to be whomever they want to be."

"Like, I want to be a soldier when I grow up?" Noah asked.

"Yes," Noah's father said. "That is exactly right."

Noah started spinning his favorite toy soldier around his finger and said, "I'm glad we're free."

"But we are free to do something much more important than that," Noah's father said.

Noah was suddenly full of wonder. "What, Daddy?"

Noah's father reached for his Bible and placed it on his lap. He then placed his hands on top of the brown and creased cover. "In our country, we are free to worship God," his father said, "and read about how much God loves all of us."

Noah looked up at his father and asked, "Is everyone free?"

Noah's father shook his head and sadly said, "No, Noah. Everyone is not free."

Still looking up at his father, Noah searched his father's deep blue eyes. He then asked his father, "What do they do?"

"Sometimes they come here," Noah's father said. "They come to America to live with us."

Noah stopped spinning his favorite toy soldier around his finger and became thoughtful. "Is that why you became a soldier," he asked his father, "to worship God?"

"I became a soldier to help protect the freedoms that God has given to us," Noah's father explained. "It's my way of showing God how very thankful I am for our Nation and everything that God has blessed our Nation with."

"Wow, Daddy!" Noah exclaimed. "You have the most important job in the whole world."

Noah's father chuckled tenderly at his son's remark. "Being a soldier *is* a very important job," he said. "But what other people do is also very important. That's why I want to protect our country."

"Daddy . . ." Noah started to say, starting to feel sad.

"What is it, Noah?" his father asked.

Noah's matching deep blue eyes filled with tears. "When do you leave again?" he softly asked his father.

Noah's father kissed the top of Noah's head and said, "Tomorrow, my brave boy."

Noah forgot about the toy soldier he was holding in his hand. The green, plastic figure dropped to the floor when Noah reached up to hug his father. Noah was proud of his father, but he did not want his father to leave again. "I love you, Daddy," he said, starting to cry.

Noah's father hugged his son back. "I love you, too, Noah."

Noah's father was hugging Noah so tightly with his big, strong arms that Noah could hardly breathe. But Noah did not want his father to let go—not ever.

S. M. Rath

## CHAPTER 2

## Noah's Promise

Noah had already dressed himself for bed when his father knocked on his bedroom door. "Noah," his father called, "are you ready for bed?"

"Yes, Daddy," Noah said. "I have my jammies on."

Noah's father opened the door and stepped inside Noah's bedroom. "Have you said your prayers yet?" he asked.

"No, Daddy," Noah said. "I was waiting for you." Noah kneeled on the floor beside his bed, folded his hands, bowed his head, and prayed aloud:

Dear God,
Please forgive me today for all my sin,
as I harbor no hate for others within.
Please bless me daily with all I need
As I live for You, grateful, without greed.
Please guide me and lead me not astray,
For heaven above is my home away.
Please help me live as You ask of me,
So, my light will shine for all to see.
And thank You, God, for all You gave
And for Jesus, who came to save.
Amen.

Noah climbed into bed and snuggled under the covers. His father sat beside him.

"Daddy . . ." Noah started to say.

"What is it, Noah?" his father asked.

"When I get scared," Noah continued, "you always give me a hug."

Noah's father wrapped his arms around Noah and kissed him on the top of his head. "That's right," he said.

"What if you get scared while you're away?" Noah asked. "I won't be there to give *you* a hug. You'll be all alone."

"I won't be all alone," Noah's father said. "Jesus will be with me. Jesus is always with me, no matter where I go. Jesus is always with you, too, no matter where you go."

Noah looked up at his father. "How do you know that Jesus is always with us?" he asked. "We can't ever see Him."

Noah's father smiled. "Press your ear against my chest," he said, pointing with his finger.

Noah pressed his ear against his father's chest, exactly where his father had pointed.

"Now, listen very carefully," Noah's father said, "and tell me what you hear."

Noah listened. "Your heart!" he exclaimed, sitting up and looking at his father. "I can hear your heart!"

"That's right," Noah's father said. "My heart is where Jesus lives inside of me. That's how I know that Jesus is with me wherever I go."

"Does Jesus live inside of my heart, too?" Noah asked.

"Yes, He does," Noah's father said. "And Jesus promises that He will always live with us here until we go to live with Him in heaven someday."

Noah pressed his ear against his father's chest again.

"What you hear inside my chest," Noah's father explained, "is the echo my heart makes every time my heart beats."

"Your echo?" Noah said. He was not sure what an echo was.

"Yes, my echo," Noah's father said. "And my echo is simply Jesus talking to me."

Noah sat up and looked at his father again. He felt delighted that he had heard Jesus talking to his father. "What is Jesus telling you, Daddy?" he asked.

"That He loves me very, very much," Noah's father said. "And as long as I can hear Jesus's echo inside of me, I know that Jesus is with me."

Noah rested his head on his father's chest with his ear pressed over his father's heart. "Boy, Daddy," Noah said. "Jesus sure says He loves you a lot."

Noah's father chuckled tenderly at his son's remark. "That He does," he said. "Jesus loves all of us so very, very much that He never stops telling us."

"Daddy, what can I do when you're away?" Noah asked.

With his arms still wrapped around his son, Noah's father drew Noah closer to him and said, "You can pray for me. Say a prayer for me every morning when you wake up and every night before you go to asleep."

"What should I pray for?" Noah asked.

"Pray that I will always hear Jesus's echo inside of me," Noah's father said. "That way, I won't ever be afraid. Will you do that for me?"

"Yes, Daddy," Noah said. "I promise."

Noah's father remained holding his son's small body in his strong arms. Soon, Noah fell asleep, hearing his father's beating heart, listening to Jesus's echo.

# CHAPTER 3

## Noah Says Goodbye

Noah was sitting at the kitchen table, trying to make the cereal floating in his bowl of milk sink to the bottom. He felt too sad to eat his breakfast. Today, his father was going to leave for his overseas assignment.

"Sweetie, hurry up and finish your breakfast," Noah's mother said. "Your grandparents will be arriving soon."

"Yes, Mommy," Noah said. He took another bite of soggy cereal and made a funny face.

Noah's mother looked at Noah and understood how he was feeling. She sat down in the chair next to him at the kitchen table. "I have a wonderful idea," she said.

Noah liked his mother's ideas. His mother's ideas always made him feel better. "What, Mommy?" he asked.

"How would you like to spend some time with Uncle Bob?" Noah's mother asked. "You two always have lots of fun together."

Uncle Bob and Noah's father were brothers. And Uncle Bob was like a big brother to Noah whenever his father was away. Noah smiled and said, "Okay, Mommy."

"Good," Noah's mother said, smiling. "I'll give Uncle Bob a call later today."

Ding-dong, chimed the doorbell.

"I'll get it!" Noah shouted as he sprang from his chair. He raced out of the kitchen and through the living room, swung open the front door, and exclaimed, "Grandma! Grandpa!" The three of them hugged and kissed each other.

After entering the house, Noah's grandfather stepped back and looked at Noah, studying him carefully. "Noah," he finally said, smiling, "I do believe you're an inch taller than you were the last time I saw you. Someday you'll be as tall as your father."

"And a soldier too," Noah said.

Noah's mother entered the living room. "Hello, Mom. Hello, Dad," she said to Noah's grandparents. "Thank you both for coming and staying with Noah while I drive Richard to the airport." (Richard was the name of Noah's father.)

"We're both happy to help," Noah's grandmother said.

Noah's father came down the stairs and welcomed Noah's Grandparents.

"We're proud of you, Richard," Noah's grandfather said, shaking Richard's hand.

Noah's grandmother gave Richard a hug and said, "We'll be praying for you."

Noah's father kneeled on the floor in front of Noah and wrapped his big, strong arms around him. "Noah," he said, "while I'm away, you're the soldier of our home."

"Yes, Daddy," Noah softly said. His father was hugging him so tightly that Noah could hardly breathe. But Noah did not want his father to let go—not ever.

After Noah's parents left the house, Noah knew that he would not see his father for a long, long time. And he began to feel afraid. He wondered if his father was afraid, too, and needed one more hug.

"Wait!" Noah called, racing out the front door. He rushed toward the car as it was backing down the driveway. "Wait, Daddy!" he called again. "Wait!"

The car stopped and Noah's father stepped out. He caught Noah in his arms and lifted him off the ground. Noah sobbed softly.

"Hey, do you remember the promise you made me last night?" Noah's father whispered into Noah's ear.

Noah nodded his head yes as tears rolled down his face.

"And what did you promise me?" Noah's father softly asked.

"To pray for you every day and every night," Noah whispered back.

"That's right," Noah's father said. "And what are you going to pray for?"

"That you'll always hear Jesus's echo, so you won't be afraid," Noah answered.

"I'm counting on you to do that," Noah's father said. He then put Noah's feet back on the ground. "Soldier," he said, saluting Noah, "take care of our home."

"Yes, sir," Noah said, saluting his father.

# CHAPTER 4

## Noah and His Sunday School Class

When Noah arrived at Sunday school, his classmates started laughing. At first, Noah thought his classmates might be laughing at him. Then Noah looked across the room and saw the Christmas tree.

*A Christmas tree?* Noah thought. *But tomorrow isn't Christmas. Tomorrow is the Fourth of July.*

Noah sat in his chair and looked at the Christmas tree. A beautiful angel crowned the top. Silver tinsel adorned the branches. And a strand of red, white, and blue lights twinkled around the tree. All that was missing were the ornaments.

Soon, their Sunday school teacher arrived and said, "Good morning, class."

Noah and his classmates stopped laughing and said together, "Good morning, Mrs. Ross."

"Isn't this a beautiful morning?" Mrs. Ross continued, smiling. "The sun is shining. The flowers are blooming. And the birds in all the trees are singing. Can you hear the birds singing outside the window?"

A few of Noah's classmates started giggling about the Christmas tree again.

"I see that all of you have noticed the tree," Mrs. Ross said.

"Mrs. Ross! Oh Mrs. Ross!" Molly cried, raising her hand in the air and wiggling in her chair.

"Yes, Molly," Mrs. Ross said, smiling, "what is it?"

"Why is there a Christmas tree in our room?" Molly asked. "Tomorrow isn't Christmas."

"That's right, Molly," Mrs. Ross said, smiling. "Tomorrow is not Christmas. But this is not a Christmas tree. This is a prayer tree. And since tomorrow is the Fourth of July, I thought that this would be the perfect time to decorate a prayer tree."

Mrs. Ross stood at the front of the class and continued, "I know that many of you have a mother or a father who is serving overseas right now. So, we are going to finish decorating our prayer tree with prayers. I want each of you to write a prayer for your mother or your father on a piece of paper. Then we will punch a hole through the piece of paper at the top and tie a ribbon through the hole."

Mrs. Ross held up a piece of blue paper with a red ribbon tied through the hole for the entire class to see. "I wrote my prayer last night," she said. "Then we will hang our prayers on the prayer tree. And every day and every night, God will read them. Even when we're busy or when we're sleeping, God will be reading our prayers."

"Mrs. Ross! Oh Mrs. Ross!" Molly cried, raising her hand in the air and wiggling in her chair.

"Yes, Molly," Mrs. Ross said, smiling, "what is it?"

"What if you don't have a mother or a father overseas?" Molly asked.

"God wants us to pray for all of our brothers and sisters in Christ Jesus," explained Mrs. Ross. "You can pray for an uncle, a cousin, or even a neighbor who is serving overseas."

"Mrs. Ross," Joey said, raising his hand in the air. Joey was always a little shy about asking questions in class.

"Yes, Joey," Mrs. Ross said, smiling, "what is it?"

"My daddy's friend is overseas," Joey said. "Can I pray for him?"

"Oh, yes, Joey," Mrs. Ross said. "All the soldiers need our prayers. And they need our prayers every day."

After Mrs. Ross passed out a piece of colored paper to each of her students, Noah and his classmates began writing down their prayers.

"Mrs. Ross," Susie said, raising her hand in the air.

"Yes, Susie," Mrs. Ross said, smiling, "what is it?"

"I want to pray for my mommy," Susie said. "But I'm not sure what to ask God for."

Mrs. Ross started to speak when Noah whispered, "Pray that your mommy hears Jesus's echo."

"What was that, Noah?" Mrs. Ross asked.

At first, Noah thought he might be in trouble for not letting Mrs. Ross answer Susie's question.

Mrs. Ross smiled and said, "Please, Noah. I'm curious to know what you meant by Jesus's echo."

Noah's classmates became silent. They all wanted to hear what Noah was about to say.

"Every morning and every night," Noah explained, "I pray that my daddy will hear Jesus's echo. My daddy says that his heart is where Jesus lives inside of him, and the echo his heart makes is Jesus telling my daddy how much He loves him. So, every time my daddy hears Jesus's echo, he knows he's not alone. And then my daddy won't be afraid."

"That is a *beautiful* prayer, Noah," Mrs. Ross said with tears in her brown eyes.

Susie stood up, walked over to Noah, and whispered in Noah's ear, "Noah, would it be okay if I pray that my mommy will hear Jesus's echo, too? I don't want her to be afraid either."

Noah nodded his head yes. Soon, all of Noah's classmates were asking him if they could pray for the same thing. Noah kept nodding his head yes while he wrote down his prayer:

> Dear God,
> Please let my daddy hear Jesus's echo today, so he won't be afraid.
> Amen.

After everyone had finished writing down their prayer, they tied a ribbon through the hole in their piece of paper and then hung their prayer ornament on the prayer tree.

Noah and his classmates admired the beautiful tree. Every prayer was for a soldier that they loved or knew and was overseas, serving God as they served their country.

"Amen!" Mrs. Ross said with tears in her brown eyes again.

# CHAPTER 5

## Noah and the Baby Jesus

**66** **I**t's Christmas!" Noah shouted, racing down the steps. "It's Christmas!" He ran to the Christmas tree and kneeled in front of all the brightly wrapped presents that were underneath.

Noah's mother walked into the room and said, "Merry Christmas, Noah!"

"Merry Christmas, Mommy!" Noah said, jumping up and hugging his mother in her pink, fuzzy bathrobe. "Can I open my presents now?"

"Of course," Noah's mother said, smiling.

Noah crawled under the Christmas tree and pulled out a big square-shaped box that was from his father. "Look, Mommy!" he exclaimed. "This one's from Daddy!" He quickly ripped away the shiny, green paper and opened the box. Inside was a brand-new soccer ball.

Noah's eyes twinkled with all the joy of the holiday. "Wow!" he said. "It's just what I wanted."

"Your father got that for you before he left," Noah's mother said.

Noah removed the soccer ball from the box and began spinning the ball between his fingers. "Now, I can practice all the time," he said.

Noah's mother gave Noah a kiss and said, "Just promise me you won't practice inside the house."

Noah giggled. "I promise, Mommy," he said.

"I'll go and make us some blueberry pancakes for breakfast," Noah's mother said.

While Noah's mother was in the kitchen, Noah sat on the floor, looking at the nativity set on the coffee table. His attention was on the manger where the baby Jesus lay sleeping. The baby Jesus filled Noah with wonder.

Noah's mother walked into the room and said, "Noah, you're awfully quiet."

"Mommy . . ." Noah started to say.

Noah's mother sat on the floor beside Noah. "What is it, Noah?" she asked.

"Why did Jesus come?" Noah asked.

"Jesus came to show us the way to heaven—our eternal home," Noah's mother explained. "And we will always know our way home when we follow Jesus."

"Mommy," Noah said, "does Jesus live inside of everyone's heart?"

Noah's mother wrapped her arms around Noah and said, "Jesus lives inside the hearts of everyone who welcomes Him."

Noah became thoughtful. "Mommy . . ." he started to say.

"What is it, Noah?" his mother asked.

"Sometimes we just need a friend like Jesus," Noah said. "Don't we?"

Noah's mother kissed Noah on the top of his head and smiled. "We certainly do," she said.

# CHAPTER 6

## Noah's Faith

**A**fter the school bus rolled to a stop and the bus driver opened the door, Noah hopped out and raced home. Noah had received his report card today, and this report card was the best one he had ever received. Noah could hardly wait to show his mother his good grades.

"Mommy!" Noah exclaimed, bursting through the front door. But Noah stopped when he saw his mother sitting on the couch, weeping, crying sadly. Her crying stopped, and she blotted her eyes with a tissue when she heard Noah enter the house.

"What is it, Mommy?" Noah asked. Noah was suddenly filled with a sense of fear. "Why are you crying?"

"Noah, sit with me," his mother said. "There's something I need to tell you."

Noah dropped his backpack of schoolbooks on the floor and then sat on the couch beside his mother. His mother wrapped her arms around him and held him close. "Today, while you were in school," Noah's mother spoke slowly and softly, "your father was injured."

For a few moments, Noah could not speak. He could not move. He sat completely still, wrapped in his mother's arms. While Noah sat there, his heart began pounding, and his eyes filled with tears. Soon, those tears began rolling down his face.

Finally, Noah looked up at his mother and asked, "Is Daddy in heaven with Jesus?"

"No, sweetie," Noah's mother said, blotting her eyes with another tissue. "But your father is hurt very badly."

Noah wiped away his tears with the back of his hands. "Will Daddy get better," he asked.

Noah's mother tried to smile. "We must all pray for your father," she said. "You must pray, too, Noah."

Noah's heart was pounding so fast now that he thought Jesus was shouting at him.

"Noah, I need to go away for a little while," Noah's mother said. "While I'm gone, your grandparents are going to stay with you. And I want you to promise me that you'll be on your best behavior."

Noah promised his mother by nodding his head yes. "Where are you going?" he asked.

"I'm going to be with your father," Noah's mother said.

Noah put his hand over his pounding heart, and he knew that Jesus was speaking to him. "How long will you be gone?" he asked.

"I'm not sure," Noah's mother said.

"When you come home," Noah said, "will Daddy come home, too?"

"Yes, Noah," his mother said, starting to cry again. "Your father will be coming home."

Noah rested his head against his mother. He listened to the echoes her heart was making. Her echoes were coming fast like his. And Noah knew that Jesus was telling his mother the same thing Jesus was telling him. Jesus was saying, "Trust Me. Trust Me. Trust Me."

Noah reached up and hugged his mother. "Don't cry, Mommy," he said. "Daddy isn't alone. Jesus is with him."

Noah's mother nodded her head yes. Because his mother was crying again, it was hard for her to talk.

Noah kept hugging his mother and said, "Jesus is our friend, too, Mommy."

# CHAPTER 7

## Noah and His Grandmother

Soon, after Noah had dressed himself for bed and said his prayers, his grandmother came in to say good night. She sat on the edge of Noah's bed. "Have you said your prayers yet?" she asked Noah.

"Yes, Grandma," Noah said. He started spinning the soccer ball that his father had given him for Christmas between his fingers. The ball was now full of scuffs and grass stains.

"Is there anything you would like to ask me?" his grandmother asked. "I know that you must be a little scared right now. We're all a little scared. But we're all praying for your father."

Noah stopped spinning the soccer ball between his fingers, looked at his grandmother, and sadly asked, "Grandma, why did Daddy get hurt? Why didn't God keep him safe? Why doesn't God keep all the soldiers safe?"

"Those are all very good questions, Noah," his grandmother said. "Sadly, though, I do not know the answers. But this is what I do know: I know that Jesus loves your father very, very much, and that your father is in Jesus's care."

Noah thought about Jesus's echo inside of his father. Noah knew that Jesus was telling his father right now that He loved him and that his father was not alone. Noah also knew that his father must have been afraid when he was hurt. Noah began to wonder if his father was still afraid now. "Grandma . . ." Noah started to say.

"Yes, Noah," his grandmother said, "what did you want to ask me?"

"When Daddy got hurt, he must have been afraid," Noah said.

"I'm sure he was," his grandmother said.

"Do you think Jesus was afraid before He died on the cross?" Noah asked.

"The Bible says He was," his grandmother said. "Why do you ask?"

"Well," Noah started to explain, "last summer I fell off my bike and hurt my arm. My arm hurt a lot, and I was afraid, too."

"I remember," Noah's grandmother said. "You had to wear a cast on your arm."

"After I hurt my arm," Noah continued, "Daddy told me he fell off his bike, too, when he was a little boy. He hurt his arm just like I did. And he was afraid, too, just like I was. After Daddy told me that, I felt a little better because Daddy knew how I was feeling."

Noah saw his grandmother's blue eyes fill with tears. "It's okay, Grandma," he said. He then dropped his soccer ball and gave his grandmother a hug. "Jesus knows how Daddy feels. Jesus knows what it feels like to be afraid."

"You're right, Noah," his grandmother said. "No one else could know how your father feels more than Jesus does."

# CHAPTER 8

## Noah and Uncle Bob

T hroughout the morning, the doorbell kept ringing. Soon, family members, friends, and neighbors filled Noah's house. And everyone who had arrived brought flowers and food for Noah and his grandparents.

Noah was in his bedroom. He was sitting on his bed, waiting for his uncle to arrive, and drive him to his soccer game. Noah was getting better at soccer, and he wished his father could watch him play. Noah's father was back in America now, but he was not home yet. Noah's father was in a military hospital. Soon, his mother would come home and take Noah to visit his father for the first time since his father had been injured overseas.

Every time Noah had asked his mother how his father was doing, his mother would always say that his father was still sleeping.

"Hey, champ!"

Noah looked up and saw his uncle standing outside his bedroom door. "Uncle Bob!" Noah cried, racing into his uncle's open arms. His uncle had strong arms, too.

Uncle Bob said, "If you win . . . ?"

Noah finished, "I'm ready to celebrate."

Uncle Bob said, "And if you lose . . . ?"

Noah finished, "I'm ready to congratulate."

"Way to go, champ!" Uncle Bob said, holding up his hand. "Give me five."

Noah and Uncle Bob slapped the palms of their right hands together high above Noah's head. Noah liked it when his uncle called him champ. Noah's uncle called him champ ever since Noah had kicked the goal that won the first soccer game of the season.

Downstairs, Noah said goodbye to everyone in the house before he left with his uncle. Noah was quiet while Uncle Bob drove his red pickup truck to the park where Noah would play soccer.

"You're awfully quiet," Uncle Bob said, glancing at Noah and smiling. "If you turn up the volume, champ, I'll be able to hear what's on your mind."

"I was just thinking about Daddy," Noah said. "When can he come home?"

"Has your mother talked to you about your father yet?" Uncle Bob asked.

Noah shook his head no and said, "Every time I ask Mommy, she says that Daddy is still sleeping."

"That's true," Uncle Bob said. "When someone sleeps for a long time—like your father—it's called a coma. Being in a coma is how your body heals itself."

"So, when will Daddy be better and wake up?" Noah asked.

"Everyone who loves your father is praying for him," Uncle Bob said. "And we're all hoping for the best."

*Everyone is hoping for the best?* Noah thought. *What does Uncle Bob mean? Jesus is taking care of Daddy.*

"Well, here we are, champ," Uncle Bob said, parking his truck.

Noah looked out the window and saw that all his teammates had already arrived at the park and were warming up. "Uncle Bob . . ." Noah started to say.

"Noah . . ." Uncle Bob started to answer, calling Noah by his real name instead of his nickname. "I know that you must be very worried about your father, but you don't . . ." Noah's uncle faltered, unable to speak another word. Uncle Bob sat with his head lowered, as if he was about to start crying.

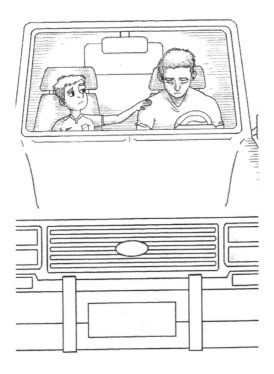

"Everything will be all right, Uncle Bob," Noah said, placing his hand on his uncle's shoulder. "Jesus is helping all of us."

Uncle Bob nodded his head yes and glanced at Noah, smiling.

Before the soccer game started, Noah said a silent prayer for his uncle. Noah prayed that Uncle Bob would hear Jesus's echo, too. He prayed that Jesus would say what Uncle Bob needed to hear.

## CHAPTER 9

# Noah and Pastor Paul

The following day, Pastor Paul came to Noah's home to visit with him. Pastor Paul preached at the church where Noah and his family went to every Sunday to worship God and to give thanks to God.

"Hello, Noah," Pastor Paul greeted, as he entered the house. "I want you to know that everyone at church is praying for your father and for you and your family, too."

"Thank you," Noah said.

Noah's grandmother closed the door and welcomed Pastor Paul to sit in one of the chairs. Noah sat beside is grandmother on the couch.

"How have you been doing?" Pastor Paul asked Noah.

"Fine," Noah said. "If I get scared or if I feel sad, I put my hand over my heart so I can feel Jesus talking to me."

"Are you talking about Jesus's echo?" Pastor Paul asked.

"Yes, sir," Noah said.

"Mrs. Ross, your Sunday school teacher, showed me the prayer tree that you and your classmates all helped to decorate with prayers for our soldiers," Pastor Paul said. "Will you tell me about Jesus's echo?"

"Well," Noah started to explain, "every morning and every night, I pray that my daddy will hear Jesus's echo so he won't feel afraid. Jesus's echo is Jesus talking to my daddy."

"I see," Pastor Paul said, looking interested.

"Jesus lives inside of my daddy," Noah said. "Jesus also lives inside of me and my mommy and my grandma and grandpa, too."

"Yes, He does," Pastor Paul said. "You are referring to the Holy Spirit. The Holy Spirit is the third person of the Trinity. Jesus also calls the Holy Spirit our 'Helper' (John 15:26 and John 16:7). The Holy Spirit helps guide us, He helps to comfort us, and He helps us to feel at peace, which you experience every time you place your hand over your heart to listen to Jesus speaking to you."

"I think that's how Jesus talks to me," Noah said.

"Indeed," Pastor Paul agreed. "Jesus speaks to each of us in ways that we will recognize His voice. In the Gospel of John (chapter 10, verse 27), Jesus says, 'My sheep hear My voice, and I know them, and they follow Me.'"

Noah became thoughtful. "Pastor Paul . . ." Noah started to say.

"Yes, Noah," Pastor Paul said, "what would you like to say?"

"I asked Grandma why my daddy got hurt," Noah said. "But Grandma didn't know why. Then I thought a lot about my daddy getting hurt, and I'm glad Jesus was with him."

Pastor Paul nodded in agreement with Noah, and said, "Before Jesus returned to His heavenly Father—after His death and resurrection—He promised to fill all believers with the Holy Spirit. In Ephesians (chapter 3, verse 17), the apostle Paul wrote that Christ dwells in our hearts through faith, so that we may be rooted and grounded in love. The Bible, which is the Word of God, is filled with many promises that confirm that Jesus *does*, indeed, dwell in the hearts of His believers." Pastor Paul smiled at Noah, and added, "Your faith, Noah, pleases God."

"Thank you," Noah said.

"Will you pray with me?" Pastor Paul asked.

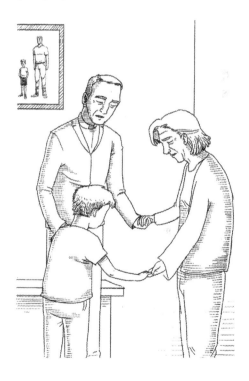

Pastor Paul, Noah, and Noah's grandmother all stood and held hands while Pastor Paul prayed aloud: "Dear heavenly Father, as it is Your will that we receive from You all that is best for us, we ask You to provide the best of care for Noah's father; we ask You to let Noah and his family feel Your love during this difficult time in their lives; we ask You to sustain their faith through the duration of this trial; and we ask You to continue to speak to them, helping them to recognize Your voice—Jesus's echo—over the voice of our adversary (enemy). This we ask of You in the name of Your Son, Jesus, whom we love and trust. Amen."

# CHAPTER 10

## Noah and His Mother

"Noah, will you come and sit with me?" Noah's mother asked. "I have something I need to tell you."

Noah came and sat beside his mother on the couch. "Will I get to see Daddy soon?" he asked.

"Yes, sweetie," Noah's mother said. She then kissed Noah on the top of his head. "But before you see your father, I need to tell you something about him."

"What, Mommy?" Noah asked.

"When your father was injured . . ." Noah's mother started to say.

Noah remained quiet, waiting for his mother to continue. Noah knew that his mother was trying not to cry.

"When your father was injured," Noah's mother continued, "the doctors were not able to fix everything. The doctors could not fix one of your father's legs."

Noah understood what his mother was trying to tell him. Noah knew that his father was missing one of his legs. He wondered, though, if his father would ever walk again.

"At first, your father will be in a wheelchair," Noah's mother explained. "But when your father is strong again, he will walk with what's called a prosthetic leg."

Noah was not sure what a prosthetic leg was, but he was glad that someday his father would be able to walk again. Maybe his father would also be able to kick a soccer ball around with him.

"Noah, do you understand what I just told you about your father?" Noah's mother asked.

Noah nodded his head yes, and then his mother started to cry.

"It'll be okay, Mommy," Noah said, hugging his mother. "Do you know how I know? I know because Daddy still has the part where Jesus lives. His heart, Mommy. That's where Jesus lives. And Pastor Paul says Jesus is our Helper. Jesus will help Daddy get better."

# CHAPTER 11

## Noah Visits His Father

Noah walked into the military hospital with his mother. Inside the building, men and women were wearing either white coats, green scrubs, or military uniforms and walking to and from in all directions. Noah was nervous about being in such a big place with so many people, yet he was happy that he would soon see his father.

After Noah and his mother stepped out of the elevator, they walked down a long corridor with many rooms. Inside each room, a wounded soldier was lying in a bed. As Noah walked beside his mother, he said a silent prayer for every soldier in every room. He prayed that all the soldiers in the hospital would know how much Jesus loved them, and that Jesus knew how each of them were feeling, too.

When Noah and his mother reached his father's room, they stopped outside the door. "Noah, I forgot to tell you something about your father," Noah's mother said. "I forgot to tell you that your father might not be able to hear you talk very well right now."

"That's okay, Mommy," Noah said.

Noah's mother gave Noah a hug, took his hand in hers, and opened the door. When they stepped inside, Noah saw that his father was sleeping.

"When will Daddy wake up?" Noah whispered to his mother.

"Soon," Noah's mother whispered back. "But we'll let him sleep for now."

A doctor, wearing a white coat, stepped inside the room. "Good morning, Maggie," the doctor said to Noah's mother. (Maggie was the name of Noah's mother.) The doctor then smiled at Noah and said, "And who might you be?"

Noah's mother said, "This is Noah, Richard's son."

The doctor shook Noah's hand. "I am very pleased to finally meet you, Noah," the doctor said. "I'm Doctor Benton, your father's physician. And right now, the best medicine for your father is lots of love from his family."

"Will hugs help, too?" Noah asked Doctor Benton.

"I prescribe at least ten hugs a day," Doctor Benton said.

"Yes, sir," Noah said, smiling at the doctor.

"Maggie," Doctor Benton said to Noah's mother, "may I speak with you outside?"

"Of course," Noah's mother said to the doctor. She then turned to Noah and said, "Noah, if you need me, I'll be right outside the door."

"Okay, Mommy," Noah said.

After Noah's mother stepped outside the room with the doctor, Noah watched his father sleeping. His father had a bandage wrapped around his head that looked like a cap. And underneath the covers on the bed, Noah could see that one of his father's legs were missing.

At first, Noah felt afraid, and his heart started pounding. What was Jesus trying to tell him? he wondered. Was Jesus trying to tell him not to be afraid?

Noah slowly picked up his father's hand and wove his small fingers through his father's larger fingers. "I love you, Daddy," Noah whispered into his father's ear.

Noah's father slowly opened his eyes.

"It's me, Daddy," Noah said. "I came to see you."

Noah's father did not turn his head to look at Noah. Instead, Noah's father kept looking up at the ceiling.

*Is Daddy looking for Jesus?* Noah thought. Noah remembered what his mother had told him. His mother had said that his father might not be able to hear him talk very well right now.

Noah pressed his ear against his father's chest. He could hear Jesus's echo inside. And he knew that Jesus was talking to his father. But because his father could not hear very well, his father was not able to hear Jesus talking to him.

"I'll be right back, Daddy," Noah said to his father. Noah raced out the door and straight to Doctor Benton who was talking to his mother.

"Doctor Benton, may I borrow your heart-scope?" Noah asked with urgency.

Doctor Benton did not understand. "My what?" he asked Noah.

"My daddy needs to hear his heart," Noah said. "He needs to hear Jesus talking to him."

"Do you mean my stethoscope?" Doctor Benton asked Noah.

"Um . . . yes, sir," Noah said. "May I borrow it?"

"Yes, of course," Doctor Benton said. Doctor Benton removed the stethoscope from around his neck, handed it to Noah, and followed Noah back inside his father's room.

"Noah, what are you doing?" his mother asked as she entered the room behind Doctor Benton.

"I'm going to help Daddy hear Jesus talking to him," Noah said as he placed the earpiece in his father's ears. He then placed the sound receiver on his father's chest.

"Your father's heart is over here," Doctor Benton said, smiling at Noah and moving the sound receiver a few inches to the left.

At first, Noah's father kept looking up at the ceiling.

"Can you hear, Daddy?" Noah asked his father. "Can you hear Jesus's echo?"

Noah's father slowly turned his head and looked at his son.

"That's Jesus telling you He loves you," Noah said to his father. "Do you remember, Daddy? That's how you know you're not alone. And Pastor Paul says that Jesus is our Helper, too. Jesus will help you get better, Daddy. Just keep listening to Him, and let Him help you get better."

Noah saw his father's deep blue eyes fill with tears. "It's okay, Daddy," Noah said, gently hugging his father. "Now you don't have to be afraid anymore."

Doctor Benton looked at Noah's mother and said, "That is a very good sign."

Noah's mother was so happy that she started crying tears of joy.

Doctor Benton looked at Noah and said, "I believe that *you* are going to be the one who will heal your father."

Noah thought about what Doctor Benton had just said

to him. "No," Noah said, "Jesus is the One who will heal my daddy." Noah placed his ear against his father's chest, listened, and said to Doctor Benton, "But Jesus wants you to help, too."

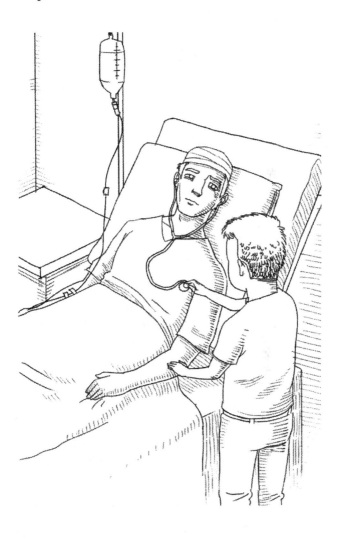

# CHAPTER 12

## Noah and Doctor Benton

As Noah's father lay sleeping, Noah sat in one of the chairs beside his father's hospital bed. Noah's mother had left the room for a few minutes, leaving Noah in charge of keeping his father company when his father woke again.

With growing fascination, Noah watched the hospital monitor hooked up to his father. The monitor looked like a small television set. But instead of a motion picture, the small screen displayed his father's vital signs: his heartrate, his blood pressure, and his oxygen level. On the small screen were different color numbers flashing off and on, and different color wavy lines spiking up and down every few seconds. To Noah, the monitor was displaying and recording everything inside of his father that God was keeping running.

The reading on the monitor that fascinated Noah the most was the pattern of his father's beating heart. Every time the green line spiked, the monitor made a soft beeping sound. Noah was sure the beeping sound was Jesus speaking to his father aloud. And Noah was sure Jesus was saying, "I'm here. I'm here. I'm here."

"Well, hello, Noah."

Noah turned his head and saw his father's physician entering his father's hospital room. "Hello, Doctor Benton," Noah said, smiling.

"Your father continues to improve a little more every day," Doctor Benton said.

Noah nodded his head yes. "God is making my daddy get better," he said.

"Yes, I do believe that God is at work in your father's life right now," Doctor Benton confirmed.

Noah studied Doctor Benton's round face. The doctor's brown eyes looked honest, but Noah wanted to be sure. "Doctor Benton . . ." Noah started to say.

"Yes, Noah," Doctor Benton said, "what is on your mind?"

"Do you *really* believe in God, too?" Noah asked.

"Indeed, I do," Doctor Benton said. Doctor Benton pulled back the left cuff of his white hospital coat and glanced at his wristwatch. Doctor Benton then sat in the empty chair beside the chair Noah was sitting in.

"As a doctor," Doctor Benton continued, "I find it hard *not* to believe in God. I have seen the power of God's healing in many of my patients."

"Like my daddy?" Noah asked.

"Yes, exactly like your daddy," Doctor Benton said. "I have learned a long time ago that my ability to heal the sick and the wounded is very limited. But God can heal everybody."

For a few moments, Noah watched his father sleeping, listening to the soft beeping of his father's beating heart coming from the hospital monitor. Noah looked back at Doctor Benton with tears in his deep blue eyes. "But

God doesn't heal everybody," Noah said. "Because a lot of soldiers get hurt and they die. And their families are very sad."

Doctor Benton's brown eyes met with Noah's deep blue eyes, and he gently replied, "Noah, God heals everyone who becomes sick or gets hurt. It is God's nature to love us and to care for us. Sometimes God will heal us here, and sometimes God will take us home to heaven to heal us. We must remember two things: one, the choice is always God's to make; and two, God will always choose what is best for each one of us—even if that choice makes others sad for a while."

Noah spent a few moments thinking about what Doctor Benton had just told him. "I trust God very much," Noah said. "And I think God wanted you to be my daddy's doctor."

Doctor Benton softly cleared his throat to clear away the lump that had quickly formed there. "Well, now," Doctor Benton said, when he was able to speak again. "Shall we listen to your father's heart?"

Noah eagerly nodded his head yes.

Doctor Benton removed the stethoscope from around his neck, stood from the chair he was sitting in, placed the earpiece in his ears, placed the sound receiver over Noah's father's beating heart, and listened. Moments later, Doctor Benton smiled at Noah and said, "Would you like to listen, too?" he asked Noah.

Noah smiled back at Doctor Benton and leapt from the chair he was sitting in. Doctor Benton handed his stethoscope to Noah. Noah placed the earpiece in his ears and, this time, Noah knew exactly where to place the sound receiver on his father's chest.

"You're already a pro at this," Doctor Benton said.

Doctor Benton remained quiet as Noah listened to his father's beating heart. Suddenly, Noah gasped.

"What is it, Noah?" Doctor Benton asked. "Or should I ask, what is Jesus speaking to your father now?"

"Noah . . .?" Noah's father softly called, as he slowly opened his eyes.

"Hi, Daddy!" Noah said happily. "You have to hear what Jesus is telling you!"

Noah quickly removed the earpiece from his ears, placed the earpiece in his father's ears, and then held the sound receiver over his father's beating heart. "Can you hear Him, Daddy?" Noah cried filled with happiness. "Can you hear what Jesus is saying to you? Jesus is saying, 'Thank you. Thank you. Thank you.'" Noah smiled at his father. "Jesus is thanking you, Daddy. He's thanking you."

# CHAPTER 13

## Pastor Paul's Sermon: Jesus's Echo

Noah was sitting between his mother and his father in the front pew at the church where he and his family came to worshiped God every Sunday. Noah was happy today. Today, his father had walked into church on his new prosthetic leg. And everyone at church had welcomed Noah's father home and thanked him for serving their country.

While Pastor Paul stood behind the pulpit and preached, Noah looked at the large stained-glass window behind the altar. The sun was shining in through the colored pieces of glass, setting the window ablaze.

In the middle of the window was a cross. The cross reminded Noah of something his grandfather had told him. Noah's grandfather had said, "The cross is where Jesus showed the world how much He loves all of us. So, every time we see a cross, we should always thank Jesus for coming and showing us the way home."

"Thank You, Jesus, for coming and showing us the way home," Noah silently thanked Jesus.

Pastor Paul finished his sermon by saying, "So, I ask all of you to place your right hand over your heart and feel the love that Jesus speaks to you all the days of your life. The spoken love that Noah says is Jesus's echo."

Noah looked up at his father and smiled. "I love you, Daddy," he whispered.

Noah's father wrapped his strong arms around Noah. His father was hugging Noah so tightly that Noah could hardly breathe. But Noah did not want his father to let go—not ever.

## CHAPTER 14

# Noah and Jesus's Message

When Noah and his parents returned home from church, Noah's father asked his son to sit with him on the couch. After Noah snuggled up against his father, Noah's father said, "Noah, I would like to ask you something."

"Sure, Daddy," Noah said.

"When you visited me in the hospital," Noah's father began, "you told me that Jesus was thanking me. Do you remember?"

"Yes, Daddy," Noah said. "I remember."

"What was Jesus thanking me for?" Noah's father asked his son.

Noah looked up at his father as his deep blue eyes filled with tears. "For letting Him help you get better, Daddy," Noah said. "So, you could come back home to us."

Noah's father remained silent; his matching deep blue eyes also filled with tears.

"Mommy says she thanks God every day for sending you home to us—safely," Noah said. "I thank God, too, Daddy," Noah added.

Finally, Noah's father was able to speak again. "Come, my brave boy," he said, smiling tenderly at his son. "Let's go outside and kick around your soccer ball."

## The End

Printed in the United States
by Baker & Taylor Publisher Services